# Dear Parent:

Congratulations! Your child is taking the first steps on an exciting journey. The destination? Independent reading!

**STEP INTO READING®** will help your child get there. The program offers five steps to reading success. Each step includes fun stories and colorful art. There are also Step into Reading Sticker Books, Step into Reading Math Readers, Step into Reading Phonics Readers, Step into Reading Write-In Readers, and Step into Reading Phonics Boxed Sets—a complete literacy program with something to interest every child.

## Learning to Read, Step by Step!

**Ready to Read  Preschool–Kindergarten**
• big type and easy words • rhyme and rhythm • picture clues
For children who know the alphabet and are eager to begin reading.

**Reading with Help  Preschool–Grade 1**
• basic vocabulary • short sentences • simple stories
For children who recognize familiar words and sound out new words with help.

**Reading on Your Own  Grades 1–3**
• engaging characters • easy-to-follow plots • popular topics
For children who are ready to read on their own.

**Reading Paragraphs  Grades 2–3**
• challenging vocabulary • short paragraphs • exciting stories
For newly independent readers who read simple sentences with confidence.

**Ready for Chapters  Grades 2–4**
• chapters • longer paragraphs • full-color art
For children who want to take the plunge into chapter books but still like colorful pictures.

**STEP INTO READING®** is designed to give every child a successful reading experience. The grade levels are only guides. Children can progress through the steps at their own speed, developing confidence in their reading, no matter what their grade.

Remember, a lifetime love of reading starts with a single step!

*For Lilly and Lucy, my little loves.*
*—M.L.*

Materials and characters from the movie *Cars 2*. Copyright © 2011 Disney/Pixar.
Disney/Pixar elements © Disney/Pixar, not including underlying vehicles owned by third parties;
and, if applicable: Pacer and Gremlin are trademarks of Chrysler LLC; Jeep® and the Jeep® grille
design are registered trademarks of Chrysler LLC; Porsche is a trademark of Porsche; Sarge's rank
insignia design used with the approval of the U.S. Army; Volkswagen trademarks, design patents
and copyrights are used with the approval of the owner, Volkswagen AG; Bentley is a trademark of
Bentley Motors Limited; FIAT and Topolino are trademarks of FIAT S.p.A.; Mondeo is a trademark
of Ford Motor Company. All rights reserved. Published in the United States by Random House
Children's Books, a division of Random House, Inc., 1745 Broadway, New York, NY 10019, and in
Canada by Random House of Canada Limited, Toronto, in conjunction with Disney Enterprises, Inc.

Step into Reading, Random House, and the Random House colophon are registered trademarks of
Random House, Inc.

Visit us on the Web!
StepIntoReading.com
www.randomhouse.com/kids

Educators and librarians, for a variety of teaching tools, visit us at
www.randomhouse.com/teachers

ISBN: 978-0-7364-8095-6 (trade)—ISBN: 978-0-7364-2846-0 (lib. bdg.)
Printed in the United States of America    10  9  8  7  6  5  4  3  2  1

DISNEY · PIXAR

# SECRET AGENT MATER

By Melissa Lagonegro

Illustrated by Caroline LaVelle Egan,
Andrew Phillipson, Scott Tilley,
and Seung Beom Kim

Random House 🏠 New York

Mater is a spy car.

Spies catch bad cars.

Spies have
secret meetings.

Spies fight bad cars.

<u>Hi-ya!</u>

Finn is a spy car,
too.

Mater helps him.

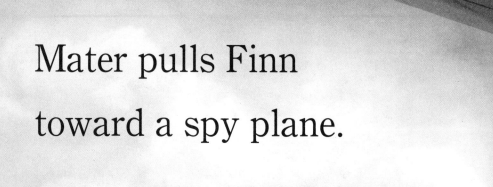

Mater pulls Finn

toward a spy plane.

# Mater learns secrets.

# Mater goes undercover.

Mater tricks
the bad cars.
He finds clues!

Mater soars away
from the bad cars!

# Mater is trapped!

# Mater escapes!

He and his friends
are in danger.

Mater and Lightning race
down the street.
Holley helps them.

# Mater and Lightning fly!

Mater solves the case!

# Mater is a hero!